"*The Planets We Become's ethereal and contemplative prose will draw you into its heartbreakingly beautiful pages. Nathaniel Luscombe captures the soul-wrenching weight of loss, immortality, and longing in a way that will have you begging for more.*"
MEGAN MCCULLOUGH
(Author of *We Could Be Villains*)

"*A haunting tale of grief, forgiveness, and the mortality of man, The Planets We Become is a short read with a deep impact. Readers will find themselves mirrored in this Dune-like story, victims of society, of duty, and to ourselves.*"
AMANDA AULER
(Author of *Daughter of the Sun*)

"*Captivating with its own unique twist, The Planets We Become is full of immersive language and an other-worldly history just waiting to be explored. Reminiscent of Star Wars, this story is perfect for those who seek depth and beauty amid a dystopian and foreign world.*"
ALISSA J ZAVALIANOS
(Author of *The Earth-Treader*)

"*It's ethereal and reminiscent of classic science-fantasy stories, with a knack for crafting destruction that forces readers to experience each moment.*"
AARON BEARDSELL
(Author of *Dead Station*)

"*The Planets We Become is an excellent sci-fi futurist mystery with an attention-grabbing plot that makes this story feel like a full-length novel. It leaves you with questions that are revealed piece by piece as the story continues. The characters in this short story are intriguing and very human in their emotions. It's a fantastic short story!*"

S. F. BROOKE

(Author of *The Strength in Rubble*)

"*The Planets We Become is a unique take on sci-fi classics, bending the 'chosen one' ideology with mythology and vivid imagery. I enjoyed seeing so much growth from the main character, as that can be rare in short stories! This is a beautiful story about hope and forgiveness and not repeating mistakes of the past.*"

ANNA FORD

(Author in *The Depths We'll Go To*)

"*Using breathtaking imagery and captivating world building, Luscombe weaves together a truly stunning short story that will linger with the reader like stars cling to the night sky. The Planets We Become is a true masterpiece of short fiction, easy to pick up and absolutely impossible to put down, gripping the reader until the last brilliant page. Do yourself a favor; READ IT!*"

ALEXANDER GRANT

THE

PLANETS

WE

BECOME

NATHANIEL
LUSCOMBE

THE PLANETS WE BECOME
A Science Fantasy Novella

ISBN: 978-1-962337-02-1

Published in Hackett, Arkansas USA by Dragon Bone Publishing™ 2024.

Edited by Cheyenne van Langevelde
Cover Design/Art and Interior Formatting by Effie Joe Stock

Dedicated to Anna Ford and Alexander Grant.

Thank you for continually believing in this story and pushing me to be the writer you knew I could be.

You're the best fans/friends I could ask for.

THE

PLANETS

WE

BECOME

NATHANIEL
LUSCOMBE

ONE

I CLOSED MY EYES, lifted my hands above my head, and focused on floating. The sort of floating that affected my mind, taking it away from the miles of sand that surrounded me. A layer of sweat coated my skin, uncomfortable like an unscratchable itch. Drops of perspiration bled down the back of my skull to the nape of my neck. They slid beneath the thin cloth wrapped around my chest. I squirmed as they crawled down my spine. It was cold against my skin and felt like a finger tracing down my spine, leaving fire in its wake.

My mind was supposed to empty itself, but I couldn't leave my skin. Every sense was heightened. My shoulder-length hair tickled like thin blades, stuck to my sweaty face. I took a deep breath and tried to blow it out of my eyes. My thoughts drifted back to the ship.

Back then, my hair had been braided past my hips. It had been a common thing for girls my age.

Cutting it was one of the first things I did to sever my connection to them.

"You can drop the pose, Rahnia," my instructor said. "I see you thinking."

I opened my eyes. The point of the exercise was to train my mind to empty itself. I was usually hit with a wave of thoughts after dropping my pose, but he was right. I hadn't cleared my mind this time.

The instructor stood in front of me. His arms were crossed, his eyes narrowed with annoyance. His shaved head bore the painted marks of power: a swirling design done in the color of blood. His pale skin was bright in the confines of our dim space. He was only wearing the traditional white training skirt. I reached out and poked a hand through his chest.

"I've told you not to do that," he said, his form flickering.

I didn't respond. He told me not to do lots of things. It felt good to remind myself that he was only a hologram. I shook out my arms, groaning in discomfort. My muscles protested at every move.

"This is for your good. For all our good. You need to be stronger if you're going to succeed." His words were, as always, clipped and straight to the point. "We'll stop the training here for today."

"I thank you for your guidance." I tipped my head forward politely, aware that every movement was being recorded. As impolite as it was to put my hands through his hologram, it wasn't something they could punish me for. Borderline insubordination, on the other hand, was. I had to guard my words carefully during our sessions.

"I want you to go out again tonight. You still haven't found any signs of the voice box, and the council is growing impatient. If I catch you sleeping before sunrise, there will be consequences."

I grimaced. My back still burned from the last time I'd fallen out of line. He had made me carry large boulders across the desert. Their sharp edges had dug through my skin and drawn out blood. I watered the dry desert with my life that night. It took the wounds forever to heal. Echoes of pain still ran through them from the salty sweat. The marks would never truly fade, and I wondered if the punishment had harmed my body more than he'd anticipated.

"I will find it," I said through clenched teeth.

"Of course you will. You have no other choice. We're all counting on you, Rahnia." His image flickered, though this time it was the dying battery. "You forgot to charge the port, didn't you?"

I threw my head back and let out a groan. I had forgotten.

"You know how important it is to keep this charged. You—"

He disappeared.

I waited, wondering if he'd come back spitting and angry in some ghostly burst of power, but the tent remained quiet. It was always so quiet. As much as I hated my sessions with the instructor, at least I wasn't alone for a couple hours. At least I had someone other than myself to direct all my anger and frustration toward.

I picked up the port and turned it around in my hands. The top was the projector and the bottom a solar panel. It was such a small thing, so insignificant in its size, but it managed to hold so much power over my life. I ran my fingers through the grooves before throwing it against the side of the tent. Instead of the satisfying crash I desired, it bounced off the material and landed back on the ground. Rage coursed through me like a wildfire, but there was nothing for me to burn.

I peeked through the tent's opening to the wild world beyond. The sky grew dark, the planet's sun making its way to the horizon. Three moons, two copper red and one pale blue, took their place in the sky. I hated everything about the planet, from its shorter days and longer nights to the sand that never stopped blowing. I couldn't wait until the voice box was found. If I could find it, this planet would become my people's. Once the planet was ours, I would no longer bear this prophesied responsibility.

The voice box was rumored to be a connection between the mortals and the gods. What gods, I didn't know, but the gods were a symbol of power and my people craved power. There was no other, solid definition of the voice box. Some thought it was a physical object, others thought it was a location. All I knew was that it was supposed to flood me with some sort of power and give me the opportunity to shape this planet for myself.

I'd heard the stories of people finding voice boxes. Each version was different, the truth split into a million pieces. I didn't know what I believed anymore.

This was not the first planet we'd searched. We followed the directions of a seer on board the ship, an odd, almost frightening person who lived in their own quarters and gave directions in return for a simple existence in peace. If that was power, the overwhelming need to be crazy and alone, then I didn't want any part of it. I was not the first of our people to come here and search for the voice box. The others had wandered aimlessly, all of them assumed dead when their contact to the ship was broken.

I was the last one from my ship to be sent down here. When I died, the ship would take a new course and haunt some other planet.

Something about this planet was different from the others. When I'd been chosen to come down here, I'd done research on some of the previous stops. This planet didn't have a large population, so establishing ourselves would not be much of a challenge. The potential for growth was immense. There was also the harsh reality that power on a planet like this was not much power at all. Not in the grand scheme of the universe. It was too dry and barren, too empty.

This was just some backwater planet, underdeveloped and forgotten.

Yet I swore the ground hummed with life.

I stepped outside, port in hand, and worked on setting it on the top of the tent. It would be facing the sky when the sun rose and by tomorrow morning, my instructor would be able to torment me again. I cast a wary glance at the moons. Somewhere between them, the station was in orbit, waiting for me to find the voice box. Once I did, they would come down to their new home. I was starting to think the voice box was a legend taken too seriously. Why would the gods leave us a way to communicate with them?

I'd grown up living an exiled life. My people were drifters. It had been a long time since one of our ships had found a voice box and taken over a planet, so long that I wondered if the gods were dead, and the voice boxes a sham.

When history is the only guide, what

room is there for the future?

It would almost be easier for me to die and let the station move on to a different, more promising planet. My people, who had grown to be more like enemies than family, were pushing me beyond my limits. Even if I did find the voice box, I didn't see much of a future ahead for me. I didn't think I could fall back into the life I'd once led, not if the planet claimed me as its own.

I sat in the door of the tent, half in my world and half in this world. All too soon, the planet would face the bare wrath of the moons, turning from a warm, sunlit desert to a cold, dismal wasteland. As the hues of pink and yellow bled away into dark, twilight blue, the sky filled with a gentle scattering of pale stars. With it came a vision of the universe as I saw it: an art piece painted for the enjoyment of those on the ground.

The ones who lived in space were not part of this covenant between the earth and sky. They didn't see the beauty of the cosmos in the way I did. From up there, it was a vast expanse of black—a cold, heartless place.

And cold, heartless places produced cold, heartless people.

It was times like this that I thought of Yoale, the boy who had stolen my heart until I'd gotten chosen to find the voice box. With his bright eyes and the curly hair that never stayed out of them, his face was the one that filled my dreams. For the first few weeks in this place, I thought of him in grief, my heart torn between love and hate. Love because I'd tried to give myself to him and hate because he'd let me go. Now, I wanted to find the voice box just so I could show him that I was worth waiting for.

My feelings for him often overshadowed those for my family. Having grown up as one of many girls, it was easy for me to slip between the cracks. I threw my love to Yoale and never really thought much of my family. When I needed them, they were there. I did my best not to need them. It made me feel better.

The oncoming breeze brought with it a taste of night. Like a playful creature, it bit and nipped at my exposed skin until I forced myself to get ready. I stepped inside the tent to grab my gear. I picked up my wrap—a large piece of material that wrapped around my shoulders—and cinched it to my waist. I tucked my knife into my belt.

I was prepared to face the world of unknown things.

I had to do most of my hunting during the night because I wasn't supposed to interact with the people on this planet. If they knew why I was here, there could be consequences. Not many people would be okay with a ship of strangers trying to take over their planet.

I breathed a quick, silent prayer to the gods of my people, more out of habit than belief, then implored the planet to lead me to the voice box. I wasn't sure whether the planet or the gods played a bigger hand in fate.

I headed out. I'd trained for this harsh survival, forcing myself to move even when I just wanted to take a break. Between the searching and the training, there was never a time when my body didn't hurt.

Every night I ventured out, I made sure to walk in a different direction. Tonight, I walked around to the back of the tent and looked toward the plateaus that rose in the distance. Their bulging heads bloomed like stony flowers from the sandy ground. There was breathless beauty to them in the bare light of the moons.

I set out, the wind sweeping across the ground with startling ferocity. I chose a brisk pace, keeping my wrap tight against my body to trap the heat. Heat was precious out here and I did my best not to waste it.

I kept a careful eye on my surroundings. The occasional shrieks of a plourhen filled the night. The small birds infested the desert, too small to be an actual problem but big enough to be annoying. One of them scurried out of sparse brush, stabbing its sharp feet into the ground to dig up a small lizard. It had taken me a while of watching them to realize that they found their prey through small vibrations in the sand. No matter how still the creatures were, the plourhen could find them.

The sand spread thin before me, and bare patches of rock lay exposed to the starry sky. Cacti grew from the rock face, their tops crowned with colorful flowers. I breathed in the sweet scent of the blossoms.

The night was more beautiful than the day. With the subdued reflections of light from the moons and the subtle smell of the flowers, it was a chilly paradise.

The shadows of the plateaus loomed over me as I drew near. I was awed by their size. I'd been avoiding them for a while. They weren't the first plateaus I'd camped by, nor the first ones I'd have to climb, but somehow, I was always surprised by their size when I stood at their roots.

I ran to the closest one and started looking for a way up. Climbing the plateaus was my least favorite part of my search, but I had anger-fueled energy coursing through me and needed a way to work it off. The plateaus had natural handholds torn into them by the wind. It was just a matter of finding the right ones.

I began the arduous climb. My hands were quickly scraped raw by the rocks. The minutes swept by. I breathed in, breathed out, my hands always looking for the next hold. Along the way, I came across small crevices that I reached my hands in. Sometimes little critters ran out, chittering angrily, and other times I got handfuls of sand.

The first hand split when I was halfway up. I winced, blood pooling in the open wound, before continuing on my way. I'd grown used to the feeling of broken skin. My wounds were a sign of hard work. They were proof I was doing my job as a seeker. My instructor judged my dedication to my quest by how wounded my hands were.

The second hand split right before I

reached the top. The skin was always so tender from constant abuse, and it broke easily beneath the pressure of this climb. I let out a string of curses, hoping it would bring the gods' attention to me. Maybe they would toss the voice box at me to make me go away.

More likely, they were watching me in amusement, laughing at my feeble attempts to find the sacred item.

This whole search for a voice box was so stupid. How was I supposed to scour an entire planet for some ... *myth*. I didn't even know what it was supposed to look like, much less how I would know it was close. Before coming here, the council had drilled it into my head that the voice box would find a way to call me.

It hadn't done so yet.

In many ways, I'd stopped listening for it.

If I paused, all I heard was the wind scraping across the singing sands. The moons reached the center of the sky by the time I rolled onto the top of the plateau. All sense of victory was drained out of me and blown away with the first gust of freezing air. It was frigid up here, the wind, wild in the space this high off the planet, threatening to throw me from the plateau.

I slowly made my way across the top of the plateau. It only took me a few minutes to search from one end to the other. No signs of the voice box. I'd checked all the holes and small caves on the way up. Nothing. I looked around desperately. My hands were burning, my legs were aching, and I hadn't even found anything. All I wanted was a little wooden post with an arrow pointing toward the voice box.

I kicked a few of the pebbles off the plateau and watched them sail through the air to the ground below. I was done with this foolish mission. I didn't care anymore.

I stood at the top of a godforsaken planet, blood running down my fingers, raw pain building in my system, foreign dust coating my clothes, and screamed.

I didn't know if I was screaming at my people or the gods. At this point I just wanted to know that *someone* was listening.

I dropped to my feet and sat on the edge of the plateau. If I was lucky, the wind would push me off and it would all be over. My people would move on, my name removed from their minds, and they would eventually settle on another planet chosen for them.

I closed my eyes and focused on breathing deep. When my body was in pain, it was always helpful to remove myself from it and focus on my surroundings. I tried to think of the wind as a calming presence instead of a gusting threat. When I opened my eyes, nothing had changed.

A shooting star crossed the sky.

Followed rapidly by another one.

Then the sky lit on fire. I watched, awestruck, as the orange flames spread across the heavens, outshining the dimming light of the stars. It was as if a huge meteoroid was falling from the sky. The atmosphere burned through them, but I could see the dark pieces continuing their arching descent toward the ground.

"What is that?" I whispered to myself. My chest tightened and my blood ran cold. The weariness in my bones was replaced with unsettled urgency. Whatever had fallen was in the direction of my camp. I crawled back to the path and started the climb down.

My bloody palms burned. I hardly gave my body a thought as I tumbled from one ledge to the next. My clothes caught on several stones and started ripping, leaving me exposed to the cold elements.

It didn't matter. I felt warm inside, burning curiosity filling me as I thought of the falling objects. The moons watched me with shallow eyes as I headed for the sandy ground.

I took off running, limping from the pain racing up my legs. All kinds of fire coursed through me. I fought against my body's protests. My heart raced a million miles a second, struggling to keep up with this sudden burst of adrenaline.

The first sign of the flaming debris was a copse of burning cacti. The flowers had shriveled. Loose flames flickered across the spikey bodies. They smoldered as I passed, wispy trails of smoke escaping into the sky. I scrunched my nose at the acrid smell.

The first piece I came across had gouged into the earth. It sat there, hot and glowing, taunting me with its strange colors. I drew as close as I could, the heat warming my skin. My breath caught. I'd seen this type of metal before. It was the outer shell of a ship.

I hurried toward the next chunk of metal. It was larger, the deep green more obvious. I knew that color as well as I knew myself. It had been the outer wall of my home for most of my life and it was the last thing I saw when my people sent me away. If the ship was down here...

...then everyone I knew was *dead*.

The thick clouds flickered with eerie light as more pieces of metal entered the atmosphere. I stepped back and watched, horrified, as the burning debris burned more holes through the clouds. I didn't know where they would land. They seemed to take forever to fall. Stars, so bright, becoming burning omens of death. I tracked them until they smashed through a dune, sending up a flurry of smoke, sparks, and sand.

I cringed at the explosion of sound. It wasn't *enough*. Here was this station falling from the sky, having held thousands of lives only hours before, and it couldn't even shake the ground when it landed.

The sky still shone, more wreckage breaking through.

My people had died, and the skeleton of my past was crumbling into its grave.

TWO

THERE SHOULD HAVE BEEN GRIEF. I would've hated myself for feeling nothing, but hate was a feeling. I hated myself and I hated my people who, gods rest their souls, had passed on to whatever lay beyond death, leaving me behind in a strange world without any reason or purpose. There was no point in searching for the voice box anymore. I didn't need a planet if I didn't have people to give it to.

I sat in the tent for the rest of the night. Occasionally, I heard the sound of debris crashing, but most of it was caught in orbit, spinning around the planet like deranged little moons. I stayed in a rigid position, the soles of my feet pressed together, and my hands held above my head. I wasn't trying to leave my body this time. I was trying to feel every bit of pain, trying to connect with everything that made me myself.

The port sat by my toes. I was waiting for a sign that this was a nightmare. I wanted my instructor to come and berate me for not charging the port. I wanted him to look at my hands and tell me they weren't bloody enough.

I thought of Yoale, the one person I'd allowed to understand me, the one I'd cried over the most when I was sent down here.

I shed my first tear. It blazed a path down my cheek and left coldness behind. I wiped it away, leaving traces of blood across my cheeks. I wasn't used to these types of emotions. Memories of my family flooded back in. They were all gone. The people I'd shared a home with for years, my mom who'd braided my hair, my sisters who'd been boy-crazy when I left, my dad who was a rigid figure in our free home.

My room was no more. The walls covered in art, the boxes full of junk under my bed, the halls that I'd once run through, the cafeteria where I'd eaten food: all of it gone.

It was all gone.

My people had been my purpose. They were a horrible purpose, but a purpose, nonetheless. Without my people, there was no need for a voice box.

Without the hunt for the voice box, there was no need for me.

So I held my hands up toward the sky, sweat rolling across my face and down my back, and thought about the future. Maybe through this pain, something would become clearer. My muscles tightened. They were wound up now, ready to do something. I waited for them to relax. The burning beneath my skin was welcoming. I could hardly feel my arms now. The blood drained from them, flowing to the rest of my body. In its place, a cold tingling began to settle.

"Send a signal to my home," I ordered. The port lit up, the hollow light of the moon enough to bring back a little power. It would try to connect with the port in the station. My heart beat faster. Maybe someone would pick up. Maybe the debris had been from another ship.

"Home is not detected," the holographic projector spoke in a monotonous tone.

Home is not detected.

Outside, another crash echoed through the plateaus. My heart shattered with it, all hope lost.

THREE

I WAITED FOR THE MOONS to sink and the sun to ascend before I let myself step out of the tent. I wanted to see the destruction during the daylight. That would make it final. The glint of the metal beneath the glaring sun, the colors stark and obvious, was going to give me closure.

I inched away from the safety of the tent. The sky seemed so bright after the fires had died away. It was cloudless, as if the heat drew all the moisture out of it.

The first of the debris lay on the ground to the side of the tent. The numbness in my body turned to a chilled realization. I could've died. The metal could've easily fallen on the tent. There would've been no chance for me to escape.

The jagged pieces were unmistakably

the metal from the station. The wind was already pushing sand over them. I reached down and picked up a handful of sand, throwing it onto the metal in hopes of burying it sooner. The breeze seemed to sense my intent. It blew harder, the sand working its way across the bones of the station, pulling them into the planet.

The desert had a way of erasing the past. Could it erase mine?

I knelt and sank my hands into the sand. Cloth was wrapped around them to help my palms heal. My fingers, though, were free, and the sand hummed with energy between my fingers.

I rested there for a moment before standing up. I couldn't bring myself to walk through the ruins. The air was thick with smoke. I took one last glance and hurried back to the tent. With the walls closed around me, I almost felt safe. Aside from the smoke hanging in the air, the harsh reality was hidden from me.

I curled in on myself, folding into a fetal position. I didn't know what to do next, so I decided to wait and listen. I would soak in the world as it moved on and hope that maybe it would find a place for me in its natural order.

FOUR

THE SOUND WASN'T NATURAL.

After three days of crying, I'd tuned myself to the world around me. I knew the way the sand shifted as the wind blew across it. Each creature had its own small footsteps, the echoes of the vibrations playing through my mind as if I was somehow connected to the ground. The light shifted around me, the passage of time marked only by the sun giving way to the moons, then the moons surrendering hours later.

But this—this sound—was something heavy. Something that didn't belong. The earth beneath it recoiled from its touch. Sand blew, wind screamed, and the footsteps continued forward. I moved my eyes and watched the sides of the tent for any signs of danger, though my body lay still on the ground.

As the vibrations grew closer, I realized I'd misread the planet's reaction. It wasn't recoiling—it was shivering with reverence. Whatever was approaching held immense power over the land.

"Please, just help me." I pushed myself up, sand running off my skin. A tear trickled down my cheek and splashed in the sand. So soft, so quiet, yet so powerful. "Give me some sort of direction."

"What direction are you looking for?" The voice came from everywhere. The ground reverberated with its power. Sand bounced between my fingers. I spread my hands across the ground. I couldn't deny the amount of power I felt beneath me.

"I need a purpose."

"I think we both know that you have always been your own purpose. Even when you were killing yourself trying to help your people, you were doing it for selfish reasons. You just wanted to be free."

"But I've never looked after myself," I cried, relieved to finally say it out loud. "It has always been for others, so many others."

"You are one of many people who have

fallen prey to others hardly big enough to be considered predators. You are a victim like so many before you."

I'd never labeled myself as a victim before. Memories flooded my mind. I remembered the way I'd been ripped from the only life I'd known, sent down here as a sort of sacrifice. All those sleepless nights where I questioned my very existence, my body broken and bruised, my mind the only part of me that felt truly alive. I thought of how even now, days after the death of my people, I was still trying to figure out how to escape them. It was true, though I'd never realized it before, that I was a victim. The word felt strange, but only because it was so *right*.

"So what now? What do I do now that everyone I know is dead?"

"You move on like you've been trying to do since they sent you down here. You're not the first to come here, and you wouldn't be the first to leave your job for someone else. Yet you keep hunting. Why?"

I didn't know. It felt wrong to give up when I had been raised thinking that those searching for the voice box were sacrificing themselves for the greater good. I wanted to believe that I was part of that greater good, that my life would have heroic, noble meaning, even when it led me to a point of wanting to die for selfish, cowardly reasons.

"I don't know anything else. Everything in my life has led up to this moment. To abandon my quest is to abandon my destiny."

"You can learn other things. I can grant you power, and the freedom that comes with power. Power might not be an answer, but it is a guide."

"What are you?"

"I am the protector of this planet—the voice box."

Was this a god I was speaking to? Some ancient deity who deemed me worthy of his words? I had to hold back a laugh. I'd once believed in helping my people, but their death had changed all my belief into unbelief. I didn't believe in the gods, and I didn't believe in the stupid voice box.

"You don't have to believe in something for it to be real." The voice still came from everywhere, but there was a distinct mortal feel to it now. I'd stopped viewing it as the voice of a god. I heard the trembles between the words,

felt the moments it paused to breathe. It was something that could easily age and crumble away.

Finality was a fickle thing. It removed the core of what power was supposed to mean.

"Have you come to hurt me?"

"I am here to change you. I will give you a purpose, though it may not be the purpose you imagined for yourself."

I hung onto his every word. I had nothing else rooting me here. Nothing except the past, and the past was dead. Ghosts weren't worth living for.

"I have chosen you for much. I expect you to get used to it. The power I offer does not come easily." Then the voice was gone as quickly as it appeared. The world felt strangely empty in the wake of all that power. The planet had always felt so alive beneath my fingertips, but now it felt quiet compared to what I'd just experienced.

Confused and dazed, I laid my head back on the ground and let the sand work its way into my hair. The conversation played on a loop in my head. All I'd gotten were more questions. I was no closer to understanding this situation than before.

I tore myself from the sand again and forced my body to move. It felt good to be up after lying there for so long. I was hollow, having let my body waste away, but that emptiness made room for something else. I'd expected to feel weak, yet I felt ready. I wasn't sure what for. I just knew this was a welcome change from the version of myself that had laid down in the first place. Though bewilderment and frustration hung heavy off my bones, a spark of life burned at my core.

FIVE

THE VOICE TORE THE TENT APART three nights after we spoke. He was quick, ripping my world down the middle with inhuman strength. My tent was made to survive the harsh elements of the desert, the material thick enough to withstand sandstorms. I didn't even have time to react, a startled scream scarcely building before the tent lay on either side of me. I felt vulnerable beneath the vast expanse of open sky.

"Why did you do that?" I sat straight, bandaged hands folded in my lap, aware of the power dynamic here. I was nothing against him.

He looked human but felt like a god. He was tall, his dark hair long enough to hang right above his shoulders. The whole planet responded to his presence. The wind was quiet for the first time that day, the sand singing louder. He smiled and reached out his hand. The air between us crackled with energy. I feared that if we touched, I would burst into flames. "Tonight, I have great things to show you." It was the voice I'd heard before, the one who told me things that didn't really make sense.

I didn't take his hand—not yet.

He stepped over the crumpled tent and sat down beside me. "What are you so afraid of?"

I met his eyes. My breath hitched. "You," I breathed, "and of what will happen when I touch you."

He slowly reached out a finger and brushed it against my arm.

For a split second, I saw a vision from above, looking down on us. A dark, silent sandstorm rushed toward us: feral and hungry, arms outstretched, a gaping maw of ravenous sand.

It went away as quickly as it came. I'd hardly seen it long enough to ponder it. His finger still touched my skin, but I didn't see anything strange now. I moved my hand to his and took it carefully, wary of what would happen when our fingers clasped.

The world remained the same.

I realized he was older than I thought. His skin felt aged, yet it was as smooth as a stone run over by sand. He was truly a desert dweller.

"What was that?" I asked.

He turned and looked toward the horizon. "A warning."

I followed his gaze and saw a storm devouring the sky. A storm that size was deadly to anyone outside. My tent would've protected me from it, but if I were to stand out in the open, the sand would surely strip the skin from my bones. A shudder ran through me. I wasn't ready to die, not like this.

"We have to find shelter," I said, even though I knew there was nowhere to go. I'd chosen this place, wanted to be so alone out here—just a girl dying in the middle of nowhere.

I cursed that foolishness now. I wanted to live—to understand this new purpose the planet was giving me.

"In order for you to change, your perception of life has to change." He let go of my hand and began walking toward the storm. "Keep up with me and your eyes will be opened."

I remained frozen. Everything in me cried out to turn and run the other way. As if I could outrun the wind. But death would feel better if I'd at least tried to live. I started slowly after him.

The wind gusted harder and the sand around me whipped into a frenzy. The planet was preparing for the power that the sandstorm contained.

"What are you doing?" I yelled as we headed closer to the tumult.

He didn't respond.

"Perhaps we should find shelter." The words were snatched from my mouth by the wind and tossed over my shoulder. I scanned the landscape for something that would protect us. There were ledges and rock formations jutting out of the ground, but none of them seemed to be enough.

They were better than nothing.

I left the man to his own fate and hurried for the nearest ledge. It was just a simple rock slanting out of the ground, leaving a small space between it and the sand. I curled up under it. The rock bit into my back.

I watched the man continue walking toward the storm. He would die in a bout of confident insanity. I was going to die a coward.

The storm's fingers reached for the man, as if to drown him, when he transformed—whatever was bound in him unleashing. The lines between mortality and divinity blurred. His form seemed to join with the wind and there was a moment where he was nothing at all, yet everything at once. His eyes glimmered and he held his arms out in front of him, embracing the ever-rushing wind. He solidified again. Maybe it was a trick of the eyes, but it was like he'd completely let go of himself. When he spun and searched for me, there was a depth to him, a deep-rooted power that so clearly resonated in every part of him.

Maybe he was a god. Maybe he was a lunatic. Whatever it was, he was no longer just the man who had torn my tent down. He was connected deeper with the planet.

The bladed tempest swept closer. In a moment, it would tear through the both of us. I just hoped it could find a place in its heart for mercy.

The two forces drew closer: a sandstorm and a man, one with tendrils of sand and the other with a single finger. When they met, the world froze.

I let out a pent-up breath. The world had not paused. The wind continued to howl between the rocks. The man had stopped the sandstorm with the touch of his finger. He turned and looked over to the place where I hid.

"Come"—he beckoned—"feel the power of the planet."

I felt foolish clambering out from beneath the stone. I hugged my arms to my body while crossing the space between us. The storm continued to build behind his touch. I felt it there, an impossible presence to ignore. When I stepped up beside him, I looked straight into the fury of the planet.

It was surreal. I stared the sandstorm down, looking at the way it moved within itself, tumbling and curling in an intricate yet scattered way.

"Don't be afraid. Touch it." He probed.

I extended my arm beside his. The moment I touched the sand, the power became a tangible thing. It was all there, so raw and ready for the taking. The sand tried to eat my fingers in vain. For once, I was the one in control.

Something akin to agony ran through me. Not physical, but mental. I pulled my hand away.

"Don't worry, you'll get used to that feeling. Power always equates to some form of pain." He stuck his hand out further and let the sand envelop it. He stiffened as he sucked some of the power out of the storm. "There's a consequence to holding this much power, but there are even greater consequences if no one does. Someone has to tame the planet. If it was left to itself, it would tear us all apart. When you hold this power, you take the energy from the planet and relieve it of the weight it carries."

"And you bear that weight?"

"Someone has to bear it. But it moves in cycles. For all the hardships that come with it, there is an equal amount of good." He leaned closer to me, and for a moment we were just two humans with the power of the gods at our fingertips. The wind grew louder, fighting against its bonds. When he spoke, I had to strain to hear. "I'm going to let it free now. It's like an animal. It doesn't like to be kept captive for too long, but as long as you treat it with respect, it will respect you."

His words barely registered in my ears before the storm leaped forward. It shot between us like wind howling through a canyon. The sound was horrible at first. It was so loud: the sand screaming in the air, the air brushing against the earth. My body buzzed with excitement. The storm had become more comforting than scary. Between its arms, I was in no danger. Nothing could hurt me.

The planet was accepting me. I had no people to call my own, but I did have the sand beneath my feet and the wind at my fingertips. Maybe that was enough. It didn't need a sacrifice from me. It wouldn't push me to do things I didn't want to. It was just a planet that would accept me as I was. My chest tightened and tears escaped my eyes. After everyone I'd tried to love had pushed me away, I'd thought I would never feel wanted again.

But a *planet* was calling me.

The storm ended too quickly. The last bits of sand rode off into the wind. I watched as it was devoured by the night, such raw power stealthily creeping across the planet. In its absence, I felt hollow. Feeling the core of the planet's power had changed me.

"Take off your bandages," the man said.

I looked down at my hands. The cloth was still bloodstained, but the constant throbbing had dimmed. I unwrapped them carefully. The skin beneath was unblemished, more perfect and painless than it had been for months. I let the wind snatch the bandages from my hands.

"How do I take this power?" I asked, breathless with anticipation.

"By becoming one with the planet."

It was just us in the middle of the devouring night; just two mortals seeking more beyond themselves. I didn't think I'd ever be this hungry for power, but having held it in my fingers, then feeling it slip away so suddenly... it was like losing a piece of myself.

I dropped to the ground, exhausted, my mind spinning. Only days ago, I thought my life had ended when the station burned through the atmosphere. Yet here I was on the cusp of unimaginable power. It was almost too much to process.

He sat across from me. "I was once in your shoes. I was sent here to find the voice box, but after a while of searching, the voice box found me. The voice box is not a connection to the gods. It's a tool that makes you something of a god yourself. The lines of technology and divinity have been intertwined here."

He held out his hands and I took them without hesitation this time. My vision expanded again. First, I watched us from above. Then, I was pulled back beyond the atmosphere. I wanted to scream, but I couldn't even feel my body anymore. I saw the planet in the way I had from the station, just a spinning orange body.

We dropped back into our bodies.

"There are so many things you can do with this power. It's up to you to care for the planet and shape it up for the voice box that will come after you," he said, removing his hands from mine.

"Why are you passing it on?" He was growing old, and this power couldn't be easy to maintain. Did I want to take something that would wear me down?

"Because I'm tired. I've been caring for this planet for *years*. I've lived a longer life than most. I was waiting for the right seeker to pass it along to, and you are the one I chose. When I pass this over, I get my freedom and you get the planet."

I wanted power, but did I want the weight of this planet? I looked around at the vast wildness completely surrounding us. Goosebumps rose on my arms. What would it feel like to be in charge of all of this? There was a part of me hungering for that control, but another part of me tried to smother that hunger, knowing I might not be the best option for a planet. "And what would I have to do as a voice box?"

"That is up to you. You can't fully understand this role until you have taken it on. It's a connection to the planet. You become its voice and you work with its needs to create a better place."

I nodded, leaning forward. "How do I accept the power?" The more he offered it, the more I wanted it.

"It's simple. I'll remove it from myself and hand it over to you. The voice box is just a small chip. Once it's in your body, it will expand and change you." He held a shaking hand up to his forehead. His fingers hesitated.

I watched him closely. I couldn't imagine passing such power on to someone else. His slight hesitation spoke volumes. "Are you sure you're ready to give the power up?"

I could've sworn I saw tears enter his eyes, but he blinked and smiled, and all hesitation was gone. "Power is only exciting for so long. Besides, all you get is the voice box. I will still feel the planet, and I think that's enough."

He pressed his fingers to his forehead and the skin split beneath his touch. A small metal object the size of a pebble slid out. The skin closed behind it. He bounced it on his palm, the entire promise of power within reach. "All you have to do is take this."

"And if I don't?"

The planet drew in a breath, waiting for his response. Conflict ran through his eyes. "If you do not choose to accept this, then my sacrifice has been for nothing. When you die, the sand will run over your bones and remove you from history. If you take it, you have the opportunity to shape this planet into something more. You're young. You have ambition. There's nothing that can stop you once you've got the voice box."

I squared my shoulders. The planet was alive beneath me, a beast seeking an owner. And I, who had always desired to feel needed, was more than willing to rule it. "I'll do it."

"First you will feel fire," he warned, "then

you will feel power. Some say they are one and the same, but those who only feel power as fire are not meant to hold it." With one hand he cupped my chin, and with the other he placed the voice box against my forehead. My body protested at the intense pain that suddenly ran between us. Every muscle coiled and I cried out. The chip inserted itself into me and my perception shifted. The pain stifled itself and turned into something more. Like cords at my hand, the planet became a puppet to my fingers. I was her. I was the rolling seas of sand, the clouds in the sky, and the cities yet unseen that rose like boils across her skin. Her inhabitants walked across me, leaving their footsteps on my skin.

Then I was darkness, a girl who could not see.

From outside my body, I watched as I fainted. The man caught me and lowered me to the ground. The connection between me and the vision flickered once, then failed altogether, leaving me to face the darkness alone.

SIX

WHEN I WOKE, the man was gone. Emptiness surrounded me. The last thing I'd seen was him holding my body. There was a bit of comfort in that, in knowing I hadn't been alone, but now the loneliness was crushing.

I didn't feel like myself. I felt at odds with my body. He'd said the chip would expand and change me, but I hadn't expected it to feel like some other being making a home in my bones. I lay unmoving on the sand. The clouds rolled across the bright sky and the planet's sun warmed me. In my head, I was processing a lot. Every part of me told me to lie still until I knew what to do next.

I felt power ebb and flow like the surging winds of the sandstorm, but it never really reached me. After the initial burst of energy, I felt like someone struggling to learn how to be in their own body. Hunger gnawed inside of me—a burning that only grew fiercer. It was how I imagined death. My breaths softened, growing shallow. I felt out of control.

I did not die, though. Even though I hadn't been eating or drinking, even though I knew my body was being pushed past its limits, there was life coursing through me.

My knowledge grew. I could feel the planet like never before. Its pains were my pains, its glory my glory. Like an earthy robe, it settled on my body as if it had always been meant for me. The dirt became my skin, the cities my heart, and the molten core my soul. The sandstorms were my anger: rushing across the land, devouring the small places before vanishing back from whence they came.

There was no rhyme or reason to the way the planet worked. It was something magical on its own, responding to the emotions that worked themselves out inside of me. I didn't speak, my throat too dry to form words, but the planet became my way of communicating.

Time lost all meaning. It flowed over me like honey, holding me fast to the surface of the planet. And amid my newfound confusion, I did understand one thing. What I'd first taken to be merely magic was actually a complex system of technology. The chip in my head was connecting me to a complex system much greater than myself.

I caught glimpses of its full power. There were seconds where I was suspended on the edge of the atmosphere, looking down at the magnificent planet as it slowly spun. Other times, I watched myself from above, taking notice at how the sand had begun to wear my skin down to the same condition that it had been for the man.

I received troubling visions of the past. They were violent and bloody, tearing into me each time I saw them.

Then I saw the previous voice box. He was still on the planet, living among the people he had once ruled. That short vision seemed to finalize the processing. When the dreams went away, I could easily call them back. The power that had stayed just out of reach was finally wrapped around my fingertips.

I rose to my feet, the wind blowing restlessly around me, and felt the planet breathe with me.

SEVEN

I STOOD ON THE TOP OF A DUNE. I'd left my old camp behind, wanting to put as much space as possible between me and my re-birth-place. The desert stretched all around me, an infinity of sand.

My heart cried for human interaction.

I had to deal with the old voice box. I'd seen things from his past that I couldn't ignore. Things he'd done. The visions of bloodlust and power were imprinted in my mind, and I couldn't unsee them. I wasn't going to leave him unattended. All I wanted now was for the planet to become a safe place. It was my home now in ways my body had never been. I was myself still, but by extension I was the planet.

I could not let him continue to live here. But I couldn't kill him either, so I had to send him off—somehow. It was a mercy he didn't deserve. I refused to follow after his power-thirsty ways.

Traveling across the planet was no longer difficult. I crouched down, pressed my hands to the sand, and felt. Like a plourhen, I could now sense the vibrations of creatures moving through the dunes. I dipped my fingers into the sand and *called*.

The ground rippled as the nearest sandstrider moved off course. They were large, hard-shelled creatures that scuttled in the belly of the planet. I stayed down until the ground opened. The sandstrider moved out slowly. It was not a pretty beast, but it listened to my words and that was enough. Having a creature listen to me was exhilarating. I'd always felt ignored, who I was brushed aside for who my people needed me to be.

I ran a hand across the creature's exoskeleton as I walked around it. I whispered promises of good fortune and long life if it would carry me to the city. The orange carapace was shiny and warm, casting the light of the sun. It dipped in the center, the plates separating down the spine. I used that as a handhold and pulled myself onto its back. My legs spread across its back, and I leaned forward, shielding my face from the sand.

The six-legged creature took off. It didn't dive beneath the sand like it normally would, choosing instead to scuttle close to the surface in an awkward, unnatural way.

It was mid-afternoon when I had called it, and the sky was growing dark when the nearest city finally appeared on the horizon. I felt the sandstrider getting tired and longing to leave. Unlike the man before me, I would not run this planet dry for my own needs. I called the creature to a stop, slipped off its back, and watched with satisfaction as it sank back into the ground.

I turned to the city. I had wanted to arrive after dark. I felt exposed beneath the light of the sun. Having avoided all cities in my search for the voice box, I didn't know the culture of this planet. From what I'd gathered from my visions, it was a strange meld of magic and modernism.

Nervousness bubbled in my stomach. I was a god-girl with access to unimaginable power, but I was about to go confront my predecessor. I didn't know what power still remained in his system. I only knew that removing the chip didn't strip him completely.

It was a comfort to know that when I

passed the power along, I too would still hold some semblance of it in the dark recesses of my body.

Hands clenched at my side and the strength of a planet behind me, I completed the rest of the journey on foot. By the time I reached the gate, the three moons had taken their positions of glory in the sky. I stood on the other side of the wall and looked for a way in.

I couldn't see into the city. The wall was built of brick, the stone worn smooth by the sandy wind. I pressed my palm to it and felt the shudder of technology running through the old city's bones. I lost myself among the cameras. They were everywhere, a lifeline between me and the city. I moved through the ones along the wall, catching strange glimpses of myself that brought upon waves of existentialism. I wasn't used to being able to see myself in such an out-of-body way. I almost felt like I had no use for my body anymore. It was but a vessel for the new being I'd become.

I followed the trail of cameras through the city. The public places were mostly empty at this hour. I saw lights through open windows and heard bits and pieces of human activity, but the city was truly beginning to sleep.

Then I caught a glimpse of *him*.

He was on a rooftop. His eyes were closed, and he looked like he was asleep, except for the fact that he was standing. He swayed back and forth to something only he heard. Perhaps he tuned in to some planet vibration I wasn't aware of.

I pulled back from the cameras and eyed the wall. It would not be hard to scale. I dug my fingers into the wall and began the quick climb. I'd found that my body could withstand far more after going through that process of becoming one with the planet. I would have to continue eating and drinking, but my needs didn't gnaw on me the way they once did.

Perched on the top of the wall, I scanned the city quickly. It was built in an interesting fashion. The buildings closest to me were the same height as the wall, but the ones nearer the center of the city rose much higher, tapering off at one particularly tall building before sloping back down to the other side of the city.

I looked through the cameras again. He was on my side of the city, still on the top of the building. With the image clear in my mind, I made my way to the first roof. The buildings were close enough together that I could jump from one to the next. The streets of the city were not wide. I used the wind to push me forward. It was almost like flying.

When I reached the rooftop where he was, I stood on the edge behind him and studied him. Though I'd spent some very important time with him, it surprised me how much of him was still unfamiliar to me. He had his face thrown back to the sky and as I drew near, I saw his mouth moving, though no sounds came out.

I didn't know how he could put himself out in the open with his sins exposed to the universe. I was a reckoning, a force of nature, and I was not here to visit.

"I know you're there, Rahnia," he said, resigned. His large eyes opened, and he turned to face me. I caught a flicker of panic, followed by a morbid sense of curiosity. He knew why I was here.

"Then you probably also know why I'm here. And don't call me Rahnia. Only my family knows my name, and you are not my family." I had decided not to have a name anymore. A name was too personal, and I didn't want it to be something that sat in the hearts of my enemies.

"Not after everything I gave to you?"

"Stop playing games with me." I tilted my chin up, meeting his eyes straight on. "When I was being transformed, I saw a history of your life play out."

He didn't have anything to say to that. The planet came to life around us, the wind whipping into a frenzy at my words. It seemed that when not under his control, the planet held a grudge against him as well.

"You killed her, didn't you?"

"Killed who?" His voice cracked. He was weak. Mortal. Easy to crush.

"The voice box before you. I saw it. She passed her power over, and you killed her immediately because you were scared she would take the power back. Is that what you expected me to do? Kill you?" My voice grew louder as I spoke, and I had to fight to keep it from shaking. I refused to appear weak, even though the adrenaline from my new-found powers was hardly enough to battle the nerves that still resided in the human parts of me. I closed the distance until we were only inches apart. "Is that what you still want?"

He shook his head. "I'd very much like to

live."

How human it was to plead for life when your actions deserved death.

"That's not all you did, though. The visions didn't show me everything, but I sensed something else. Something big. What was it?" I spit the last words out, daring him to try to lie. I saw the answer on his face before he spoke, and a dangerous mixture of sorrow and anger rushed through me. I restrained myself, waiting for him to admit it out loud.

"I destroyed the station."

The words were a punch to my gut. I almost stumbled back, everything in me begging to put more space between us. Nausea wormed in my stomach.

"It's how the previous voice box got me to take her position, and it's partly why I killed her," he continued, desperate to explain. "She said it was what all voice boxes had to do one day. I didn't quite believe her, but when you came along, it felt like the right thing to do. You hated them." He threw that last sentence on as if to justify his actions.

I raised my fist. He turned his face away, expecting some sort of death blow. I wanted to kill him. I wanted to reach my fingers into his seams and tear him apart. But I couldn't face the person I would become if I began using violence in that way. I lowered my hand and tried to think of something to say.

In killing my people, he had tried to give me the thing he thought I'd wanted: power over myself. What he didn't realize was that I never wanted my people to die. No amount of anger could justify the deaths that had happened. Just as my anger now couldn't justify me killing him.

"What do you want me to do?" I asked, bitter. How did I have the power of a planet at my hands, yet still ask someone like this for directions? I was lost. I'd never meant to shoulder this sort of responsibility.

"Let me live. I don't want to die. I am not ready to face death." His voice trembled. He'd left his divinity behind and turned to a life of technology, still trying to find a way to keep himself safe. His absolute fear of death had to be connected to the horrible things he knew he'd done.

"Then you have to leave," I said harshly. "I won't have you living on this planet anymore. Not with the things you've done. I'll take care of the transportation. I don't care where you go as long as you don't come back here."

"You would kick me from my own home? The home I gave you?"

I understood the pain. He was going to be ripped from the place that had once been his body. Just as I now dwelled within the planet, so had he. "I could do worse." I wasn't backing down. This was nonnegotiable.

I saw the surrender in his eyes. He nodded. I mentally reached up into the atmosphere where several transport pods hung in orbit. They were one of the first things I'd discovered when exploring the limits of my power. They were waiting to be used.

Now one would escort this man to whatever place he wanted to call home.

"A transport will arrive tomorrow. I'll send you to whichever of the nearby stations you'd like. If I ever catch you returning, I'll send you away again. In pieces."

He didn't bother arguing. I watched him leave the roof, presumably to pack. I would come back tomorrow to make sure he went onto the pod, and when it departed, a part of me would trail it to the station to make sure he really left.

This was the first time I felt fully in control of my destiny. I was settling into my role as the voice box and even though I'd just dealt with confrontation, I felt peaceful.

EIGHT

I BECAME A RULER in the absence of the previous voice box. Without his presence, there was no one left who knew what I was capable of. It allowed me to explore my abilities and change the way the planet was run without interference. I was a woman who knew no bounds. I closed the divides between the people, threading peace between their wicked words, and led them into a golden age.

Civilizations rose and fell beneath the shifting sands, but humanity never stopped coming back. Countless years went by. The moons continued to cycle; the sun continued to shine. All was as it should have been from the start.

Time blurred together. I was present at times, living in cities and learning the ways of the people. Other years, I stayed out among the plateaus and sandstriders. I spent nights raising sandstorms only to calm them, trying to befriend the planet. I'd throw myself from plateaus and beg the wind to catch me. I'd search the skies for my replacement, knowing that one day there would be someone new seeking the voice box.

But I wasn't quite ready to hand over my power. Not yet. I wanted to revel in this existence for just a moment longer. Even when those moments turned into millennia. Even when my bones felt a bit heavy, and my soul craved the eternal rest of death.

The planet was a home to me. I learned to know every nook and cranny. It wasn't a big planet, and I could travel the whole thing in just a couple years, scaling mountains, visiting cities, never growing tired of the dunes laid out before me.

The planet being a complete desert was pure poetry. I was myopic in my existence. In a never-ending sea of sand, I felt comfortable in every spot. Sometimes I would lay in the sand for days at a time, letting it work its way across my skin. I felt alive in the hands of the planet. It never stopped singing. Its very core hummed constantly. I lost myself in the notes, never alone even when the nearest cities were days away.

It was easy to forget I was once only human, that this power was really just technology. I'd wake up craving interaction and make my way to whatever city or village came next, if only to make sure I still knew how to use my voice.

I heard my legends pass through the mouths of strangers. I'd sit at the inns in cities and listen to the gossip. I was nameless, a woman with no roots, and it was beautiful. They spoke of my kindness; they spoke of my justice. The same woman who devoured a wicked village in sand was also the one who found reservoirs of water for thirsty cities.

It was the balance I'd sought to build.

I wanted to set the planet up for success in my absence. I knew that one day I would have to move on like all the others before me. I didn't want whoever continued my rule to begin with the mess I'd started with.

Then they came. The ones I knew would be seeking the next voice box. So many years had passed since I'd accepted this role and the planet had finally experienced peace. I'd lost myself in that time, unable to count the years that had passed. I was growing weary beneath the pull of power. When the ship brushed against the shield of technology protecting the planet, I let it through. I watched carefully as a pod broke free.

Even from the ground, I could feel the anger radiating through the metal of the pod as it soared through the atmosphere. What a strong emotion anger was. Once, I'd been that angry—just a confused child sent to do an adult's task. Whoever was in that pod didn't feel like a stranger to me. They were more like a mirror, or a window looking into my past. I wanted to welcome them off the pod and wrap my arms around them. I wanted them to know that everything would be okay.

But I held back. I couldn't risk passing the planet over to someone who would ruin it. I'd have to be picky. Even if it meant watching someone fail at their task and die.

I remained distanced from the landing site. The pod was a star falling from the heavens, a streak of orange in a dark blue sky. The jets along the bottom ignited and the pod jolted back up, going from an uncontrolled fall to a careful landing.

I did not approach with my body, my inner being hovering around the ship as a boy stepped out. He was so young, barely into his rebellious years. Tall, muscular, a sort of awkward surety built into his body.

I stuck by him for days. Driven by desperation and pain, he hunted night after night for the voice box that would free his people.

I was the past keeping an eye on the future. I couldn't change what the previous voice box had done to me, but I could change the way I treated this new one. I would stop the cycle of death that wrapped this planet in a crimson shroud. In order to do that, I had to get to know this boy. I had to know he was the right choice to continue carrying my power and responsibility.

I thought briefly of the other man who'd handed me the power. How did one live through so much and not grow a greater sense of empathy and kindness? I was determined not to follow in his footsteps.

So I waited and watched and learned.

He was not bad. He treated the planet with more respect than I had, always careful in his hunting. There were times where I did approach in body, remaining just out of sight. I liked to see this search for the voice box through another perspective. Watching someone else pursue a power that they didn't even understand was so intriguing. To think that I had done that once was wild. It was a past so far removed from me, I could hardly picture myself back here.

The cameras never forgot. I let them rewind and watched pieces of my own hunt. I was uncomfortable seeing myself as the old voice box had seen me. The girl in those videos was nothing like the person I'd become. It had taken many years to come to terms with the path of my life, but looking back at where I'd started, I could only be grateful that I was the one chosen to carry this gift forward.

So much had changed in my lifetime. Granted, it was a life that extended beyond its normal years, but as I watched my younger self, I wanted to reach back through time and just let her know she was going to be okay.

I no longer lived my life through the weight of other people's eyes. I wasn't pursuing a purpose thrust upon me. I was taking the hope inside me and planting it in the world around me. There was a time I hadn't cared about anyone other than myself. Even in hunting for the voice box, I'd only done it because I needed the validation of my people. I'd grown a lot from that person, becoming genuine in my need to better myself and my surroundings.

The past was exhausting. It was then that I realized how badly I wanted to live a normal life for a few years before dying. I was ready to hand the power off.

I just had to do it in a way where he wouldn't kill me in the process.

NINE

I WAITED UNTIL THE SEEKER had given up on finding the voice box. His hunts had become more a routine than anything else, his hopes growing smaller. Some nights, I thought he was going to pack his belongings and head to a city. He could start a new life down here apart from his people if he wanted to.

Only when he grew hopeless did I know he would be willing to listen to what I had to say. He stopped venturing far, sticking mostly to his tent. I watched him one evening, just a lonely figure staring at the stars ... or perhaps searching the stars for a sign of his ship. When I'd thought of my people, it had motivated me to keep hunting. He didn't move and that's when I knew he was ready to listen.

I emerged from the plateaus, making my way across bare stone, bits of sand blowing around me. I made sure he could see me approaching from a great distance. When he spotted me, he shot to his feet. He was set up for the night, his tent already erected behind him and a fire crackling at his feet. He kept the leaping flames between us as I drew near. He tracked my approach with sullen eyes. His fists were clenched, his body rocking back and forth as he prepared for a fight.

"Who are you?" he asked.

I liked that he spoke first. It showed his confidence in his ability to stand his ground.

I studied his startling blue eyes and dark hair that ran over his ears. He was a beautiful man, and it was a shame he'd been thrown to the planet to find the voice box. I knew what turmoil must rage within him right now. I just wanted to help him unleash it. Only when he let that anger go could he begin to heal.

"I am the voice box," I said, holding my voice steady. I had never spoken those words before. It freed up space in my chest, the weight of this secret sliding off my ribs.

He looked me up and down. I knew how I must appear to him. I was no longer young, and one could even think I was weak. I'd lost control over my body while trying to hold the reins of the planet. He snorted and turned away. "Alright then. You expect me to believe I was kicked out of my old life to find some old lady?"

I settled down on the other side of the fire. It had been a while since I'd closed the planet out of my mind and focused on being human. Putting up that wall left me feeling uncomfortably vulnerable. I wanted to connect with him in this moment as just a person. I couldn't let my power get between us.

But he was filled with disbelief, so I lifted a wrist and called forth the sand. A dust devil bloomed behind me. I spun it with motions of my finger, watching as the young man made the correlation. For the first time in all these years, I was able to show off my power.

I'd never realized how *proud* I was of my power. I'd spent an extended lifetime learning the tricks to controlling a planet. Moving the sand with my mind barely scraped the surface.

He eyed me carefully now, a hunter looking at its prey. I mentally reached out toward him and felt the bits of excitement flow off him like the glowing stardust on the tail of a comet. He was a man who'd just found the answer for his people.

I'd never had the chance to do that.

I broke then, humanity overwhelming divinity until I was a sobbing mess in the sand. I was acutely aware of the young man watching me in confusion, just as I was always aware of my surroundings in some way. Even with my eyes closed, I wasn't blind. I still saw my surroundings from an out-of-body perspective. The fire crackled, my tears buried themselves in the sand, and a lonely wind screamed behind us.

He finally moved, crouching before me, and tenderly taking my hand. His own hands were broken and scarred from training. I remembered the days when I'd come back from hunting, bleeding and broken, my mind numb to the pain. Somehow, his brokenness, akin to my own, made me feel whole.

"And why would the voice box, the most powerful being on this planet, be crying?" he asked gently, a tentative grin crossing his face.

I sniffled and wiped my eyes. "Because the voice box isn't what you think it is. It's not a connection to the gods—it's a connection to the planet."

"Are they not one and the same?" He stretched his free arm out, gesturing at the wildness around us. "Planets are pieces of the gods, the pieces they choose to share with us."

I shook my head. "It's not as simple as that, though. If you accept the power of the voice box, you'll spend several lifetimes trying to balance power and pain. I need you to understand that. I took this without knowing the cost. If my family had come down here, I would've watched all of them die of old age. I'd exist among their generations, unconnected and lost. If you'd rather disappear into a city and make a life for yourself beyond your family, I'd respect that and wait for someone else."

He considered my words. "Was this power forced upon you?"

"Not forced, but I didn't think I had much of a choice. If I could go back though, I would still take it. I just know this life isn't for everyone. I don't want to feel guilty passing the weight off to you without giving you the choice. You have to accept it freely."

"If I take it, my people can make their home here?"

He didn't know the history of this planet, the long lineage of voice boxes tearing ships apart and forcing power on emotionally vulnerable seekers. I was glad to shield him from that.

"Your people can move down here, but they have to be willing to live in harmony with the planet. I won't give you this power so you can force this planet to live beneath your family's rule. I'm giving it to you so you can care for all of us." I looked up at the ship in orbit. It was small and couldn't have been carrying more than a couple hundred people.

"My people just need a home."

"Do you feel that they've been fair to you?"

He looked at me carefully, as if trying to guess what sort of response I wanted. "I think they've done the best they could with what they have," he finally said.

"Good. Remember that. This power is not a tool for revenge. I don't think you should take out any anger on your people. I felt that anger when you arrived, and I've been waiting for it to die down."

"Did you take your anger out on your people?"

I shook my head, then realized it was actually my entire body that was shaking. "Someone else used my anger against my people and forced me to lose them. While there was a bit of relief at first, I've been breaking over it for years."

That confession set something off within me. Like the sands sliding down the dunes, my soul slipped between my ribs and sank into my stomach. I felt nauseated from the grief that overwhelmed me. A sandstorm in my lungs, knocking me forward with emotion.

It felt necessary to get that out. It had been easy to forget the horrible death of my people. I never had allowed myself to dwell on it. Knowing that the sadness still existed in my body meant I hadn't fully lost touch with what it was to be human.

He held me in his arms. I marveled at his compassion. When I'd been in his place, I hadn't had compassion for anyone beyond myself. He was a better human than I had ever been, and I could only hope he would also be a better god.

"I don't know what you've been through or exactly what you're asking me to do, but I will do everything I can to help you." It was probably the first time he felt he had a choice in helping someone. It was not a purpose forced upon him but an opportunity he chose to take.

That made me feel content.

TEN

His name was marel.

When he asked me for my name, I told him I didn't have one and explained why I'd shed it a long time ago. It was easier to care for the planet when its inhabitants didn't know who I was.

He brought me to meet his people. The ship broke through the atmosphere and came down slowly, circling around until it came to land before us. It was alien in this sandy wasteland. The planet was on its best behavior. The wind played gently with the sand, sweeping it across the ground in a beautiful display. It pattered against the silver walls of the ship.

His family were the first to step onto the new planet. They surrounded him, excited, supportive, and he seemed to have forgiven them. Something I never got the chance to do.

I hung back, a little bitter. Not at him, but at life. It was so unfair that I'd had to take the pain of my hunt and sow peace from it. I was happy to see the reward, but I wished I could've had a voice box like me, who cared and loved the planet, in place of the man who'd ripped my life away.

Marel introduced me to his family. It was only his mother and three sisters. From what I'd gathered, his mother held a position of authority on the ship, and it was why he'd been chosen to search for the voice box. They all looked so alike, their features smooth, their eyes gentle. Perhaps I'd misread this situation. It was likely that not all who hunted for a voice box were under the same unrelenting pressure as I'd been.

More of his people gathered at the top of the ramp, waiting to take steps down to their new home. I beckoned to them. They hung back behind Marel. They were a timid bunch.

I didn't think I'd have to worry about them mistreating the planet.

"Welcome to my planet," I said.

Their eyes turned to Marel. He flushed a little. "She hasn't given me her power yet."

The eyes came back to me. One old man looked me up and down. "Show us, then. Your power, I mean."

A chorus of agreements rose. I laughed a little. There was no harshness behind them, just a lot of curiosity. I lifted my arms and called up a cloud of sand that filled the air behind me. My physical movements were for show, as I could control it all without moving.

I just wanted to impress them.

"Once he's ready, I will take Marel away for a few days and train him to take this power."

His people pushed him forward, as if they were anxious to get settled. They seemed ready to begin preparing for their new life here. But they treated the entire planet with caution, not rushing out into the open spaces. Marel still stood between me and his people, a body bridging the gap between the power in my veins and the frailty in theirs. I heard his mother speak softly, telling Marel to be careful around me.

"Marel tells me you're planning to build your own city," I commented.

"We would like to live peacefully here.

We mean no harm to anyone as long as they don't harm us," his mother said. "We prefer to stick to ourselves. We would like to not be a burden to you or anyone else."

I turned away to hide the tears gathering in my eyes. It was almost cruel that the universe had sent such a lovely group of people to take over my life's work.

Marel came up behind me. "Are you okay?" he asked.

I grabbed his arm. "We should go. I'm turning soft. I think I should retire."

He laughed loud and hard at that.

I led him away from his people. The sooner we got this over with, the sooner I could breathe in relief, knowing that the planet was in good hands.

ELEVEN

WE FOUND A QUIET PLACE out in the middle of nowhere. I couldn't help but feel transported back to the time I'd received the chip. Back then, the world was tense and ready for battle, wrought with sandstorms. This transfer couldn't be more different. Though I felt his body shaking slightly, he was more prepared than I'd been. The planet was soft around us. Our feet sank into the warm sand. I'd gotten used to walking across my own body, my human form but a vessel.

I was scared of feeling lost without this connection.

I'd warned Marel about what would happen when I transferred the chip. The pain was such a distant memory for me, but the transformation that had come after the pain would never completely leave my mind. I couldn't forget how the planet went from being a soul-less desert to a close companion.

"Are you sure about this?" I wanted to give him a final chance to pass this opportunity.

"I've never been more sure about anything," he responded firmly. "Let's get this over with." He knelt down in front of me.

I'd always worried I wouldn't know how to pass the power on, but the instincts took over as if the planet, too, was ready for a new guardian. I held my fingers up to my forehead and the chip passed painlessly through my skin. I'd expected more, even just a ghost of the pain I'd felt while accepting the chip.

How hollow the world felt for a moment. I'd truly lost connections with everything. The sand was quiet, the sensation of other life gone. Before I could overthink it, I passed the chip into his forehead. Though he made no sound, his eyes rolled back, and he passed out from the pain.

I held tight to his body, laying him down carefully. He would be the type of leader the planet needed him to be. The one who would act with compassion, even when given abili-ties that could remove morals from his mind. I thought back to the way he'd treated his people, putting them ahead of himself. He didn't have the same bitterness as me. Nor did it seem his people had pushed him like mine had pushed me. He was going to be a leader with a strong community as a foundation. It was in that moment when I knew for sure I'd chosen the right voice box.

My mind struggled to accept the confines of my body. Where once I'd felt endless, I now felt trapped. I could feel the planet's life around me, but I couldn't tap *into* it. I wouldn't want to live for long like this. Death was overdue. I just wanted to stay around for long enough to be the guide that Marel needed.

The guide I could've used when I first started.

I left his body in the sand. He would be okay. The planet would transfer what memories he needed, and when he woke, he would have more than enough to think about. If he ever needed me, I would always be in a place he could find me.

I retreated to one of the cities and watched the planet develop under the hand of a new voice box.

When the time was right, the planet would call me to my final resting place.

TWELVE

I DIDN'T FEEL LIKE I lost *all* connection with the planet. While I couldn't move it at my will anymore, I still felt the echo of its tremors as it fought for survival. Maybe it was my imagination giving me what I longed for, but it was comforting, comforting to not be completely alone.

Marel took my place easily. In most ways he was a better ruler than I had ever been, but I still gave myself credit for changing the ways of the previous voice box.

Living in the city was not easy. I felt trapped behind the stone walls, the desert winds never free between the buildings. I felt older without the world there to support me. The wind didn't stand behind me. The moon never shone in my favor.

And when the planet finally called my

name, it was on the day that Marel came to tell me he had found himself a wife. She was from his ship, a girl who had been his since before he was called to search for the voice box.

I knew then that my job was done. He would no longer need my guidance. He had found his place in life, and it would guide him forward on its own.

I swallowed hard while congratulating him, forcing the thick emotion down my throat. "I loved a boy once, you know. Out of all the things I've lost, love has been the hardest."

Marel looked at me, expecting more, but there was nothing else to say. He knew what had happened to my family. I'd told him about the sins of the previous voice boxes.

I had no place in the universe anymore. It had all been taken from me.

"You're ready to die, aren't you?" He didn't meet my eyes. He was good at reading people. I'd made it clear that I wouldn't be around for long, and I was glad he picked up on it before I had to speak it out loud.

"I am." I spoke with surety. There was no room for doubt now, or even resignation. Death was the natural next step in my existence. "I will begin my walk tonight. When the planet sees fit, it will send a sandstorm my way and I will give myself to it."

He pulled me in for a hug. "Thank you for everything you've done."

I held him tight. Even if I was ready to die, it wasn't easy to let go of the things I loved.

"Are you scared of death?"

"I was once, but I know now that I've given all I can in life. There's nothing left for me here. You've taken on your role well and you're able to make your own choices now." I leaned back and patted his cheek, unable to do more. My body was heavier without power, age digging into my bones like rot. "Do one last thing with me. Bring me up to the roof so we can watch the moons rise."

He nodded, struggling to keep the tears from his eyes. We left my small home behind and walked up the stairs to the roof. Each step was a struggle, as if my body had heard my declaration of death and was already giving up.

We stepped out into the open, and a million memories swept over me. When I looked at the desert, I thought of those days when I lay in its hands, the power changing my body. I remembered finding the old voice box on a roof much like this and forcing him off the planet.

I held Marel's hand tight, and we sat down at the edge of the building. Just a former god looking over her world one last time.

We watched the orange sand roll in the wind. The sky turned red as the cycle of night drew near. The orange moons edged their way into the sky, and I watched their ascent for the last time. The blue moon was still making its way over the horizon. And somewhere in the desert, a sandstorm was being birthed, preparing itself for my death. For one, final time, I would become one with the planet.

LETTER TO THE READERS

EVERY WRITER MUST, at one point or another, write a story that shocks them.

The Planets We Become was the first story I wrote that felt out of my control. When I finished it (mind you, the first draft was SO different from any of the published variations), I had to sit back, relax, and let the story settle in my mind. It was so much more than I'd meant for it to be. Coming to terms with what I'd just written was a fun yet nerve-wracking process.

This is the story that taught me so much about writing. When I got an editor for it, I was feeling quite proud of my work (I almost hadn't hired an editor). I approached it from the perspective of it being a perfect piece that didn't need much adjusting.

I was wrong. Obviously. I'm sure every writer has felt this before, then had their dreams crushed when they got their editing notes back. There was a lot to change. Not only was the writing a bit messy, but the plot had to be chopped up and certain scenes had to be removed to get rid of a message I hadn't considered being present.

It was a scary yet important process for my writing.

That was back in 2021. It's now the end of 2023 and I've just finished rewriting this book with the intention of finally releasing a version I'm really happy with. I know this book will never please everyone. It's strange and unique, with some odd narrative styles thrown in that feel more experimental, but I'm always going to like the way this story turned out.

I'm glad to finally be releasing a 'final' version of this story. It has been published four times now ... and I think it's tired. I'm just glad none of the other versions ever became popular. If people are going to read this story, I'd like it to be this version.

I look forward to writing something new now! Hopefully something just as fun and shocking, and hopefully something that's longer.

If you really loved the desert sci-fi vibes of this but wanted something longer, I recommend checking out my book *Moon Soul*! I think *The Planets We Become* paved the way for *Moon Soul,* and even if that's all this story ever is, it was well worth it.

IV

ACKNOWLEDGEMENTS

ANNA FORD AND ALEXANDER GRANT: you're the driving force behind every 'final' version of this story. Whenever I think of this book, I think of the two people that pushed me to believe in it. Thank you for all your love and support. I wouldn't be excited to share this story again if it weren't for the amount of time you've spent convincing me it's worth it.

Effie Joe Stock: thank you for taking my old story and helping me dust it off. I owe so much to you. Thank you for the art, thank you for publishing it, thank you for being such an amazing friend.

Cheyenne van Langevelde: thank you for editing this story and helping me strengthen its voice. Editing with you is always a joy.

All the people that have read and enjoyed this book in its various stages: thank you for making time (and money) for my stories. I know I haven't always delivered the best quality, but I'm working on righting my wrongs and I am so excited to be moving forward into a future where I only publish the best things. Those of you that have supported me from the beginning, I wouldn't be taking the steps I am without you.

Last but not least, my family: thank you for being big and loud, but also leaving me alone so I can write my stories. I look forward to all my siblings being old enough so I can guilt trip them into reading and buying my books.

MOON SOUL

A *Cozy Science Fantasy Novella by*
Nathaniel Luscombe

DISCONTENT COMES SO SUDDENLY.

The pain of daily living is catching up to me. I've hit a point in my life where I can't ignore it. I wake up dreading my existence. I want to close my eyes and never open them again. It's hard to function this way. I go through the motions without understanding why I bother.

I guess I find comfort in filling that role. It's there to keep me on track. I want to be more than on track. I want to thrive. I want to be ... happy.

When I was seven, my father told me that he chose my name after a season on Earth. August. It's a long month, one that brings in the end of warmth and the beginning of cold. I couldn't help but take that to heart in a way they didn't intend: I began to view myself as an end.

It didn't help that they separated only a few months later, though it was less of a separation and more of an abandonment. My mother wanted to go back to her life in the desert. My father couldn't follow her there.

I can't help but think that the end is my only destiny. Everyone dies, but is everyone only destined for death?

If so, we live a sad existence in a cruel universe.

Signed,

one who does not know who they are

ONE

I SPEND THE NIGHT struggling to rid myself of emotions that are not my own. They're remnants from my day, little pieces I've picked up from the sand. It's exhausting trying to deal with them. How does one process something that does not belong to them?

I pace across my small room. On days like this my home feels like a cage, even though the outer walls are made of glass, opening to a breathtaking view of Argysi. Each time I pass, I touch the glass, trying to send some sort of feeling into my body—something that is my own.

The hardest part of absorbing other people's emotions is feeling things I have never felt. Today, I worked with two customers seeking memories of their parents. The intense love I felt conducting the emotions opened a black hole inside of me. I no longer have two loving parents and perhaps never did, making all my memories of love a sham. I'd been abandoned by both, even if one abandoned me because I told him I no longer needed him. It hurts nonetheless.

I crave love, but I want an organic form, not someone else's leftovers.

My eyes burn. I have been crying for hours, trying to drain the excess emotions. I'm sure there are red rims around both my eyes, and my cheeks feel crusted from the dried tears. Unable to do anything else, I settle against the glass and succumb to the overwhelming feeling of everything.

I feel the heartbeat of the Spire pounding around me. I'm on the ninety-sixth floor, only four floors from the top. The walls around me carry stories. I feel the gentle hum of the machinery within the Spire and the vicious winds rattling the glass, and beneath it all I hear the calming sound of music serenading my neighbor to sleep. I let the thrum fill me for a moment. In the Spire, we are only as good as our counterparts.

I wonder if anyone around me can feel my body shutting down.

«◇»

THE BLOOD DOESN'T COME until I've left my apartment and gone to the roof. Every Spire has a publicly accessible roof; the ledge circling it is where the gardeners drop down from to work in the gardens that hang around the outside of the Spire. The Spire doesn't have rules against coming up here, just as it doesn't have many firm rules about anything, but it's an unspoken rule most people are fine heeding.

I stand as close to the edge as I dare and look out over the moon. Blood trickles out of my nose. I press my wrist against the flow, trying not to let it drip. I don't want anyone to wake up and find their windows splattered with blood. Despite my efforts, a few drops wrap around my skin and fall, only for the wind to splash them back in my face. I laugh, then grimace. The blood is warm on my skin.

The view of Argysi is the only thing keeping me calm. I hold a deep, aching love for this moon. It's the only aspect of life I enjoy, yet contact with it is why I'm up here. Why does it, with its beautiful, purple sand and sweet breeze, have to be the source of all my pain?

I walk to the spigot where the gardeners get their water and turn it on. A drain eagerly laps up the bloody water as I stick my arm, then my face, beneath the cold stream. I scrub at the blood. I can't tell if it has stopped flowing, or if the water is washing it away too quickly for me to notice. I breathe through my mouth, sucking in the fresh air.

I open the small shed sitting beside the spigot. On the inside, rows of harnesses hang on lines of hooks. I grab one and begin putting it on. The first time I did this, I'd struggled with figuring out how to adjust the straps. Now, it's almost second nature to pull it over my shoulders and clip the rest around my body and under my legs.

The gardeners use these to move up and down the tower. I often watch them from the ground. When they're near the top, they're nothing more than bouncing figures in the wind, possessing that wild freedom I crave.

Unlike the gardeners, I don't have the energy or skills to climb up and down the building. I just like to sit on the edge knowing that if I fall, the harness will catch me. I crouch down carefully, sliding my legs over the edge and letting them dangle. Pain dances across my soles. Just looking down makes my stomach feel funny. I embrace the discomfort. I'm here because of other people's extreme emotions. I think I need some of my own to counter them.

I take comfort in the fact that from this height, I can see Argysi's flaws. As with any moon, it's pockmarked and scarred from the space debris it shelters Oviun from. The green planet is hard to see at night when the dark colors fade into the universe, making it visible by the lack of stars in its place. It's an emptiness in the midst of everything else.

The universe above me, the moon below me, and me—stuck in the middle. I don't know who I am or who I should be. I am a being made from other people's feelings.

I don't think I can justify it any longer.

I'm going to quit my job.

MORE FROM
DRAGON BONE PUBLISHING™

ANTHOLOGIES

Aphotic Love: An Anthology on the Depths of Romance

The Dragon Bone Journal (2024 Issue)

FANTASY

Child of the Dragon Prophecy (Book 1: The Shadows of Light)

Heir of Two Kingdoms (Book 2: The Shadows of Light)

Bleached Reminders: A Gothic Anthology about Bones, Magic, and Grief

SCIENCE FICTION/FANTASY

Moon Soul: A Cozy Science Fantasy Novella

The Planets We Become

CHILDREN'S BOOKS

Turklet, Squeaky, and the Seven Chicken Chicks: Love Overcomes All

Milton Keynes UK
Ingram Content Group UK Ltd.
UKHW041805180124
436252UK00001B/7

9 781962 337021